Bad, Bernie!

Written by Paula A. DiVincenzo

Illustrated by Jubayda Sagor

To our Bernie and Brutus for making "bad" look so "good". You put a smile on our faces every day. Love you to the moon and back! And to all of the dogs in need of loving homes. You are all the inspiration behind this book.

-PD

Bad, Bernie!

Mommy and Daddy said it was love at first sight.

Mommy would call me her little "Chubba Wubba" and give me lots of kisses.

Then, one day, things started to change.

Mommy and Daddy would yell when I was in the bathroom. "Bad, Bernie!"

Mommy and Daddy would yell when I chewed up their new carpet.

"Bad. Bernie!"

Mommy and Daddy would yell when I would play chase during walk time. "Bad, Bernie!"

(I really didn't like that leash I tell ya'!)

Mommy and Daddy would yell when I chewed wood chips and rocks outside. "Bad, Bernie!"

"Bernie, we think it's time for you to have a companion to play with," Mommy and Daddy said to me one day. "Doesn't that sound like fun?"

What's a companion? I thought to myself.

"Bernie, meet Brutus. Your new little brother!"

This "new little brother" tried to play with me, but I wasn't having it.

He even tried to play with my toys! I hid them in a corner.

Mommy and Daddy would yell, "Bad, Bernie!"

One day, I decided to try something new. This "bad" stuff was really starting to get on my nerves.

I shared my favorite toy with Brutus. Mommy and Daddy cried excitedly, "Good, Bernie!"

Wow! I thought to myself. I like the sound of this! *Let me try again!*

I gave Brutus a few kisses. Mommy and Daddy picked me up and gave me the biggest hug you could ever imagine!

"Good, Bernie!" they cried.

I decided from that day forward that GOOD was a word that made me feel GREAT and I didn't want to be so bad anymore.

The real Bernie and Brutus.

Made in the USA
Middletown, DE
27 October 2017